LOVER'S ROCK

a these americans love story

Cover Design: Neda Aria

A Blue Max Publication

301 Alten Ave NE. Grand Rapids, MI 49503

KDP ISBN: **9798340339027**

Ingram Spark ISBN: **979-8-3305-1114-3**

FOR NEDA

SPANISH BOMBS

It wasn't as though anyone was watching. It was seldom anyone was. Those were different times—times before social media and cell phone cameras. Historical archives of debauchery were left to Polaroids, thrown into a box that you didn't throw out but never looked at.

The world was less of a stage in hindsight. There was less accountability for a failed performance, and reviews were left to gossip among the people who kept the information close. How far could it spread anyway? Nope, the living reminder of clusterfucks was left to a person's distorted version of the truth.

Unless you were Gus.

Gus had truly little self-control, but did have Tina and a conscience—I guess you could call it a conscience. And Tina? She was a sort of karmic reminder that one's personal view might be somehow warped. She was like a Dickens ghost or Clarence Odbody. She popped up at seemingly random times to remind him who he was.

You also felt as though she was your angel only, and an angel to nobody else. From Gus's point of view, she was an angel only for Gus. There was no contrary proof of Tina existing outside of the tiny bursts of introspective interactions between the two, anyway.

So, were they fucking or not? Were there rumors floating around the coffee shops, bars, and campuses? Were the baristas and bartenders whispering about them? Why would they?

I suppose during those bursts of spontaneous conversation, they might appear to be fucking, or brother and sister—it depends on the viewer's personal history or imagination. I would assume they were fucking or married. These are two undoubtedly different things. I suppose one might lead to the other. Maybe for them.

Gus often wondered if Tina was even real. His friends joked that she was imaginary, and the fact that she never appeared when they were around only deepened his doubt.

To Gus, she was one of the most beautiful women he'd ever laid eyes on, much less talked to. To Gus, the dynamic, while conversing, removed sexuality from the mix entirely. He really only obsessed over her body, her lips, and her accent while at home— at night. Sometimes at work or a party, he'd think about her lips and her body and her face. When sitting with her, her scent, the way she moves in her t-shirt and combat boots, the thoughts took a hiatus. He wanted her all right. But he also really, really liked her.

There is a problem though. When young Gussy thought about Tina, he didn't truly think about *her*. He selfishly placed her as his, entirely, and never considered that she had a life outside of their timeline together.

When they were apart, he wondered, *What should I do?* or *What is she thinking about me?*

It was rare for him to ask, *What is she doing?*

This was a result of not crossing the line into love or sexual obsession (yet). Let's not forget, she had a way of putting Gus in his place. The whole fucking thing was confusing. Wrong time, wrong place, wrong fucking era. —Maybe.

Till now, Gus never recognized her pain.

Koka Kola

It was 3:30 am when Gus pushed open the door of his shitty apartment on the Northeast side of town. He was still alive, so it seemed, but oblivious to the workings of keys. His brain fired off bursts, like polaroids, random acts of debauchery that led up to this 3:30 am arrival. Maybe not debauchery. Maybe just fucking off. There were bits of shirtless dancing and bits of wrestling and bits of odd or blurry talking about sad things or smatterings of memories from the prior weekend that were made to be reminiscent and somehow sentimental. The same smatterings that Tina would absorb and reflect Gus in a more embarrassing and less sentimental light— vampiric fear than lack of one's own reflection. Oh well, who doesn't arrive home at 3:30 in the morning and an absolute disaster several times a week? Even still, Bukowski would… right?

So, all these bursts of less-than-photographic moments ran about Gussy's head until his head hit the pillow. This is when all those bursts spun up into a swirling void that consumed the body and made it impossible to flutter to the bathroom. He did make it to the bathroom. There was nothing that could save him, save the cold tile floor and cold condensation aside the bowl. For this reason, Gus would remain there until, after several sessions of exorcisms, he'd sleep there. He would break with the morning in bed, unsure of how he had made it there and with most of those Polaroids, from the evening's events, lost to the darkness. He had a class to get to.

CAREER OPPORTUNITIES

Even art school was a challenge for Gus as he forged his way toward his illustrious future bartending career. Partially color-blind and void of any ability to focus on anything, Gus trudged on, bull-doggin', with a long-instilled mindset of dying before 30, or at least trying to.

Like all the other things in his life, he didn't put forth enough effort, or focus, to make it happen. So, he smirked, critiqued, and infatuated and assimilated, fueled by movie quotes and song lyrics and the occasional half-ass attempts at being funny. He produced very little art but maybe just enough to get by with a decent grade. The college was urban and most of the extracurricular activities took place on the sidewalk, side-door nook—two or three cigarettes, and a cup of coffee, dreaming about love. Restless.

It would be of great disservice to the school and its impressive curriculum if we did not mention the great gatekeeper who served as a buffer between the real world and all those color classes and still life classes and robe-wearing, life-drawing models in the small school elevator.

That great gatekeeper, her name was Patti, and she'd sat there for what would be four lifetimes to a young student. She was robust with short red hair, styled up and molded with hairspray, shaping her ears and whatever large and brightly colored earrings adorned her blushing round head. She was average which made her above average in the imaginary world of art school.

Patti watched soap operas on her lunch break and would talk about them with anyone. She South-Beach dieted while making light of her weight. She was down-to-earth, with an 80s hangover, and with a quick wit and a self-deprecating but contagious laugh. She was down-to-earth and could hold a conversation with anyone who needed an ear. She was every student's mom away from mom.

"Morning Patti," Gus would say, every single day.

"Look at you! I take it you had another rough night, Gus?" she'd say.

"That's what coffee's for."

She'd chuckle that contagious chuckle, smile that contagious smile, cheeks lifted with blush. This made any unreasonable morning suddenly reasonable.

The walk to the coffee shop from the free parking is a good four or five blocks out of the way—a long way to go with a hangover. This was worth the trip, should Gus walk into the coffee shop, and find Tina sitting at a table, drinking a chai and reading or writing. The odds that she'd be there were against him, as he'd never actually run into her before a morning class. Though he knew she wouldn't be there, he went anyway. It was the only real thing to look forward to on most days and, there or not, the anticipation was the reward. This was the end of fall, days before Halloween, and it was cold and dry and might snow at any time.

     Aaron Paul Schaut

The coffee shop routine had become a thing after classes too. Gus played roulette with three coffee shops that supported asshole eccentric artists like him. This particular afternoon landed him at The Black Hole where he sat, smoked, and thought on dreams. His Kerouac sat in front of him, as though he would read, and his coffee would cool with the chill breeze brought on by the big door opening and closing. Young artsy couples wander in for their cozy drinks before a night of scrabble, making Halloween costumes, and enjoying gentle sex.

She didn't show up that afternoon.

This is when Gus begins to really dive into his lucid dreams and subconscious perceptions. *Maybe she wasn't real. Maybe I'm making it all up. Why do we keep running into each other and why don't I ask her out or something? Maybe we could be lovers— all dressed up for Halloween. He isn't that. She is probably not that. What of it?*

He wrote an abstract poem in his journal Just then. It wasn't like the other garbage he'd written.

Perhaps it wasn't him that wrote it, but instead, the moon, guiding those Silvertone words, from that expensive art school pen, onto a page. He'd let himself be taken over by its shimmery light.

He felt older as he wrote. Like an older man begotten by a muse. Some Hemingway bullshit.

His knee was bouncing up and down. He could feel his dad smacking him in the leg and yelling at him to *stop*! He couldn't help it. Hyper—he couldn't breathe.

While he felt the urge to sit and wait, an entirely silly act, he also felt a strong romantic breeze had taken hold of him. —Something Gus was proud of, known for, or needed to be. He was always envious of those moments in the movies when the rush took over. Something in the method. Marlon Brando and James Stewart and James Dean and all of that romantic desire pulsating through the film. Silvertone anger and rage and lust and love, tearing through the silver and making you *really fucking feel it*. No, Technicolor wasn't required when it came to pushing the boundaries of the Hays Code or the MPAA or whatever thing was creating the rules. Without the rules to break, would the message be so strong?

He read the poem to himself. A surge of passion ran through him. It was written as a means to say something. Maybe he could share it—someday—with her. Maybe it wasn't a poem at all, no, it was a feeling, in color—as bright as little ol' Gussy could shine. If he were to share? Silvertone would do just fine. Maybe she'd suffocate?

I'm So Bored With the U.S.A.

A week had passed, and Gus had made a trip to the Upper Peninsula to visit Mom and become consumed by the thought of a relationship that was broken apart upon his move to the city. In a similar fashion to those GR coffee shop dreams of Tina, he would roll around Escanaba in his big, shitty car, hoping to stumble upon lost love. The still-familiar faces around town, brimming brightly with excitement upon seeing Gussy cruise by, would undoubtedly end up at some bar, reminiscing about the "old days"—being a few years prior. All those churned-up, young, troublemaker blues that led to this or that or the other thing. Ah, the things that a teenager can get caught up in while in a small town. The Boss, that boss, could write a song or two about it all, but the story would lack the bravado of the honest man.

So, one story went, Gus, Bubba, Beaver, and a kid named Aaron would roll up and down Main Street as everyone else did in the late '80s or early '90s. This was the tail end of the American Graffiti America from the '50s and '60s. The big yachts with wheels affixed to their underside slid, growled, and scraped. Thunderous bass resonated through loose license plates, causing arrhythmia while shaking loose any old rust. Bubba was behind the wheel, while Beaver sat shotgun, having cooked up a plan to launch Roman Candles at whatever group was cruising with their windows down. So, there was this little Mustang GT packed with guys glaring and girls snarling, and their windows were wide open. Beaver lit that Roman Candle and *poof, poof, spit, shriek*, the little balls of sparks and flames launched around and into the Mustang.

This... this would bring on what you might call the reason for it all. Bubba slammed the gas pedal to the floor of that Monte Carlo, speeding off for the fire roads next to the train tracks and boat yard. This was a dirt road with ruts, and he'd get that thing up to 80 miles per hour without so much as a flinch. That Mustang (or Mustwang as some said) would be right up on their bumper with almost no visibility, as all that sand and dust ripped up from behind the Monte.

That trail would rip right into Bubba's turf in North Town. Bub cranked the wheel into a scrapyard full of sharp curves and even bigger ruts that could easily send a car into an old dishwasher or engine block. The car jolted, and Bubba nearly lost control. One of the rear tires had caught a piece of scrap metal that pierced its sidewall. With Beaver grinning, Bubba rode that car with the fury of the General Lee but with one wheel riding on the rim. They rolled that rim all the way to the alley behind the tire shop. A quick snip with the bolt cutters got them a brand-new tire in the trunk. A few blocks later, Bubba sat at the wheel, honking the horn outside the high school auto shop garage door. The door opened, and ol' Clem, the shop teacher, stood there looking calm—think Daryl from Newhart. Bubba rolled into the garage, said he was going to swap out a tire, swapped the tire, and the four were on their way to McDonald's for however many cheeseburgers they could buy with whatever money they had. All of this was as casual as it gets—a normal night in town.

Gus didn't run into Bubba or Beaver or any of those guys, nor did he run into his ex. He did run into a club night at what was the old Delft movie theater, converted into a bar and dance floor, and figured, why not? He parked, went in, and knew everybody there. The club was a new thing in town, and as new things go, everyone went. It was strange to hear music in a club in Escanaba that wasn't made by C+C Music Factory or Boyz II Men.

Gussy moved about the club drinking vodka tonics, hugging, dancing, and dreaming. The old stage in front of the movie screen—the same screen where he'd seen Return of the Jedi—was full of people twirling and grinding. The screen itself served a visceral reel of trippy 3D effects and kaleidoscope swirls. Gus moved around the stage, confident if not pretentious, now from the city. A lot of the crowd were also visiting from the city or some college campus miles away.

At the end of it all, Gus, a bit drunk and a bit ambitious, gave one last tour of Main Street before leaving those ambitions of the ex behind and rolling back to his parent's house. Stumbling into bed, his mind wandered back to the ex, back to Tina, and he missed his new home in the city. He wanted to wake up on his mattress in his little apartment, wander into Music X or The Black Hole, and wait for the future to present itself. Little did he know that this waiting would become long-term. Tina was probably waiting for him. But why would she? He was not there. He couldn't shake the thoughts and got up and outside, lighting a cigarette with the flick of a Zippo. It started to rain, and a single drop caught the end of the smoke. He let himself drown.

I Fought the Law

Gus, after hugging goodbye, with Mom standing in the driveway watching him leave, made his way toward the highway, leading home. Slowly, what had been a depression and sadness was changing and evolving into excitement and possibility. His U2 mixtape fueled a growing desire to take the highway and the city by storm. As he neared the Mighty Mackinaw Bridge, his anxiousness bled into his gas pedal foot and drew the attention of the police.

"Where's the fire?"

Do cops actually say this? "Um… I'm sorry, officer. I saw the bridge, and this music was playing, and I guess I got a little… um… overstimulated."

"Yeah? Well, the bridge isn't going anywhere. License and registration."

Gus turned off the U2 and let himself crawl the rest of the way to the toll booth. After the bridge, on the interstate, he'd let it all loose again. *Fucking cops.*

Lover's Rock

1999. A year later. Grand Rapids.

She tasted of spice and sugar and set him on fire. The memory of it imprinted on his skin and soul as if the burn and sting of a tattoo remained constant. Spice and sugar. She smelled of spice too. If fragrance chemists could capture the scent of Djarums and chai latte mixing with her natural self, and bottle it? I'd buy them all.

It was a cold November night. Gus, nearly defeated by the depression of winter looming, a third desperate attempt to reconnect with the ex, and the holidays not close enough to ignite any spirit, made a last-minute run to X for a coffee, hoping to run into Tina. He could see from a block away that the place was empty. His jaunt slowed, but nevertheless, he headed toward the door. To his surprise, she had met him there at the entrance, looking up at him, big, beautiful eyes peering through the hood of her hoodie. He swung open the door and gestured for her to enter. Seven Year Bitch blasted off the walls and windows as the two ordered their drinks—a chai for her and a coffee for him.

Gus didn't know what *this* was. He longed for her but was somehow paralyzed from pursuit. He had the confidence, or at least he always did in the past. Why wasn't he chasing after Tina? Why wasn't he blasting her with charm, begging for her, pining away all hours of the day? Did she intimidate him that much? Maybe it was the accent or something about the way he always felt small around her. Her snarky belittling, while fun, had Gus in a constant state of questioning his actions and thoughts. He thought of her as an angel, and like the Catholic Church, she made you pay for your sins. Sin was certainly on his mind. Gus wouldn't call it sin, though—he also wouldn't say "sex." To Gus, it was love or "making love." There wasn't any "fucking" in Gus's world. He tried that once and still felt a disgusting guilt about it. To Tina, this was probably "immature," but to Gus, it was engrained on his core. Odd little words that can define the meaning

 Aaron Paul Schaut

or purpose behind actions. Fucking is boring—making love is eternal—passion is the sweet fragrance of love's blossom. Bottle that up too.

Yup, something about Tina made Gussy shy. Maybe this meant it was bigger than what Gus had thought of that big old word, love, thus far. Maybe it wasn't. Oh, Gussy, sweet, sad Gussy, your heart will pump all this melancholy into your brain, and you'll smoke and drink and try to make sense of it all. Until you have some sense, you'll pine enough. You'll seek her out and make her your everything, and she will stay just far enough away to keep it confusing. She is, after all, Tina.

Mongo Bongo

Roger watched a small gecko scurry up the wall of the adobe house that Gus and Lily made their home.

"Leave it," Gus would say to Roger, so many times a day. Roger knew the command and pouted into a sploot nearly every time.

Gus sat at the patio table, smoking a cigarette and sipping coffee while staring blankly at the dirt and sand that served as their backyard landscaping. After the move, Lily had quickly become connected to the Albuquerque scene. It never took her long to integrate—all that charm and charisma that separated her from her peers.

The immediate need for money had her working most days while Gus worked nights at a local watering hole called Pete's. The work schedule was tough on them. The reality of routine had taken a back seat to all the love-sick, find-the-girl, leave-the-guy drama of the prior year. The routine is when things fall stale. Either way, the day/night shifts either helped or hindered the romance, while the routine would surely kill it.

Gus tossed an old tennis ball into the gravel for Roger to retrieve. Roger just looked at it. He, too, had forgotten the disappointment and torture of his past life. The routine had gotten to him too—made him a lazy dog.

Gus put out his cigarette and lit another before grabbing his phone and messaging Lily.

[We should visit Stacia and Chick. We should go to GR.]

He stared at the little "Delivered" notice below the message. That little message haunted him as a reminder of all the delivered messages he'd sent Lily so many times while she was gone. That's a lot of fucking reminders on any given day. So, with unnecessary anger, he typed "?????" and hit send as though the button could feel his angst. Then, as if his terror-rage had landed a Tyler Durden blow, "Delivered" changed to "Read."

[WHAT?] She responded.

Gus put the phone on the table and looked at it while squinting. "Fuck that," he said out loud, as though the phone would understand. He took a hit off the cigarette, then, apologizing to the phone like the weak asshole he was, typed:

[Nothing. It's cool. We'll talk about it later. Xo.]

[Delivered.]

Let's Go Crazy

November of 1999 (Last Kiss)

It was cold, rainy, and wet—all the things that made Gussy stir-crazy. He and Tina sat in Music X, listening to "November Rain" on split earphones while drinking coffee and solving the world's problems. They'd drive around those oil-soaked streets, searching for signals of futures bright with dark satire and black comedy. Gus joked that they should stop into the Cini-Mini on Leonard and catch a flick. *Cini-Mini was an adult theater known for its glory.*

"You wish," Tina chortled, smiling, knowing full well Gussy did make those wishes.

"You know what's better than porn?" Tina raised an eyebrow as she asked.

"Chinese food?"

"Brad Pitt's abs."

"Fight Club?"

"Please?"

And they rolled up Alpine and hit the Star Theater like two crows, playing Mr. Jones on the radio, separated only by an armrest.

Gus, being Gus, always trying to escape reality and encourage a liquid bravery, thought it'd be fun to whiskey up with Tina during the movie. The place was mostly empty, and they sat in the back row as was Tina's usual request. The projection light flickered above their heads while they shared some smuggled-in candy with their theater popcorn and soda.

Gus felt warm from the whiskey, but more so with desire. She was right there next to him, and the tension, the electricity, and all those things that are so often used to describe desire, made each second last a lifetime, while surreal space-time, dark matter, pushed toward something deeper. The porn at the Cini-Mini could never capture the nature of chemistry. If it could, they'd be lined up around the block.

Gussy fidgeted, inched, charged particles surrounded hands barely separated by thinly scented air. Only a few times in Gussy's life had he felt this indescribable, pulsating attack make its way through his entire nervous system. Yes! He would file this moment away in his brain, and heart, as 'times he's been truly impacted by love.'

He could feel her resistance, like magnets that push and pull, and all of it prolonged any anxiety by adding a pinch (or punch) of doubt.

Her eyes on the screen, with that flicker about them, set their own scene that Gus could watch endlessly. *No need to respond*, he thought. "*I can do this all night*," he whispered. She heard him say it but pretended not to.

The whole scene was all broken up when Kim Deal's ominous voice, with the delicate strumming of an acoustic guitar, filled the theater with the appropriate lyrics for the moment! *Where is my mind?*

This is where we are.

Gus snapped into a reality that never fails to collapse the scene when the theater lights come up.

Leaving the theater, the rain fell in big plopping drops, strong and bold like Gus's come-ons (right). In the car, the space between them was loud while they sat quietly ignoring the tension. Gus put away any logic and fully ripped. "Let's hit Gardella's," steering toward the bar and away from potential rejection. She didn't say no. The rabbit said yes. Anxious adrenaline took over. A strange bar illuminated by garbage illuminated strands and old booths. They had a corner away from the groupings of bachelors and bachelorettes looking for a screw. Drunken, sunken eyes—different from Gus's and Tina's. Ralph Lauren hunters just blowin' off some steam or some shit. Smelled like the fucking mall.

Gus tossed some money into the jukebox and played some R.E.M. after ordering shots and beers. His ears heard the ringing taking over. He'd lost his ability to gauge anything. Attempting to flirt, James

 Aaron Paul Schaut

Dean drivel came out of his mouth. Some cooked-up Johnny Strabler line like, "You ever just do something 'cause it felt right?" Tina paused—maybe offended at the idea that he thought she hadn't. All Gus was really looking for was a sign to make a move. A little hint that the whole thing wouldn't play out with him spiraling alone into oblivion. Tina played along though. The movie script was spot on. Two rebellious kids on a mission. Two kindred spirits looking for meaning, reason, life, and love. Two strangers being strange together. But were they strangers? Nah. They had joked about being the same person in a parallel universe. Perhaps they were a figment of each other's imagination. Maybe an imaginary friend or one of those god-damned pookahs. Lord knows that stranger things had taken people in America. These Americans—all bound up with irrational rationality, rationed just so. Always pushing for that universal dream. *Think about all these things, Gussy. Do it with a buzz and while simultaneously focusing on stealing a kiss and a heart. Yeah, that's us in the corner, eh? Michael Stipe?*

Stop!

Gus reset at the sight of her sitting there at the booth. Big eyes and sugar and spice. Rational and irrational. It didn't matter. It was all soft—all right there. She could have been from Tehran; she could have been from Kalamazoo. It didn't matter. "Gates of the West" came on the jukebox. Gus fell into the booth with a smile.

"What's so funny?" she asked.

"You are," he smirked.

"Well, that won't get you anywhere."

"But I have a car," he leaned in a little.

"You're lucky that the thing gets you a block."

"You should talk."

"You talk a lot." She took her shot.

"And you're scary." He drank his.

"I'm Persian." She put her shot glass onto the table upside down.

"But can you dance?" *This was it!* He took her hand and led her to the little dance floor. "Think you can keep up?" Madonna's "Ray of Light" lit the place up. Gus flailed around while the Persian moved like she'd been a backup dancer in videos.

She pulled him in close. He smiled and laughed, and she sensed his shyness. She pulled one of those classy dance twirls, and he almost tripped over himself. Their faces just an inch apart, she teased him. Had he become some kind of prey?

Some guy with a saxophone came up to them wailing some jazz solo. He put his hand out for a tip. Tina gave him some skin, looked at Gus, and winked. Gus gave him a buck.

She took Gussy's hand and led him out of the bar. The rain fell hard, so he took off his blazer and placed it over her shoulders. He did this. He thought about how he wanted to be a little closer to the holidays. He wanted to be "that sentimental holiday Gussy." He leaned against the wall under the eave and lit a cigarette when a car sped by through a massive puddle. "Gus, you're drenched!" Tina laughed so hard that she snorted. He tossed his wet cigarette to the sidewalk and smiled that big, dumb Gussy smile that she maybe loved.

Here, David Attenborough might say, "The prey had finally signaled to its predator that it had become vulnerable. For the predator, it was worth the wait. The coaxing had paid off, and the prey would become the unfortunate victim."

She grabbed his wet face with both hands and pressed her lips into his. The rainwater and the chilly air enhanced the sensation. He put his cupped hand on the back of her head, and she slid hers around his neck. Blood rushed through every part of his body. For Gus, this was a rare occurrence with a first kiss. This moment, he'd carry it with him, forever.

     Aaron Paul Schaut

"Unbridled passion," Attenborough continued, "would consume both the predator and its victim. Perhaps, in this case, the predator had become the victim. This species is a complex one, and the tides can turn on a dime."

"Fuck off, David Attenborough!" Gus said aloud.

Tina pulled away with a "What?"

Gus pulled her in tight, the rain soaking their core. "Nothing." He lit another cigarette and handed it to her, and they stared into the oily street. "The Sharif would not be pleased," he said with a sad smile. She smiled a little and softly hit him in the chest.

David Attenborough: "It's best to forget any awkwardness of the night's end. So, the night had come to an end, and so had the rain. Perhaps both Gus and Tina had become the victims. Either way, they would cohabitate in a small abode without consummation. For Tina was far too drunk to drive home."

Coma Girl

A little bit into the future. Albuquerque, NM

Gus was already working the bar while Lily settled into a glass of wine and the couch. She was thinking about the text he'd sent earlier while feeling lonely and tired.

As if the world could sense a rift in space-time, her phone belted the last note of the X-Files intro. It was a text from her best friend, Stacia. Stacia and her partner, Rae—who goes by Chick—had opened a successful taco joint, settled down, and had just been approved to adopt a little girl. They are throwing a little adoption party and want Lily and Gus to come to Grand Rapids.

Like with Gus, Lily wouldn't respond immediately. She was becoming overwhelmed with life. Being tied down wasn't in her nature, and while she knew full well that this was her own problem, she felt the urge to flee. It's been less than two years since she last fled, and nearly a year and a half since she learned her lesson and made the commitment to

Gus, to her friends, and to herself. She put on a PJ Harvey album, the one Gus bought her for Christmas, in an attempt to reflect on herself and find peace. She knew she had Gus on edge but had no idea that Gus, in his own way, felt the same. It was as though neither of them could embrace each other without the tragedy of losing each other looming—a masochism disguised as tragic optimism.

She stared at her phone with that wine in her hand. She loved Gus tremendously, and she knew it, and he knew it, albeit both of them had guardians. They were able to completely and totally go all-in, even though those built-in or youth-instilled reactionary walls were both tragic poison and necessary guard dogs. Yet, it appears that somehow, in the wake of all her tragedy, two people found stability and love—enough even to add to their family with a child. Lily couldn't imagine what this must feel like. For her, there is no stability, even in times most stable. New Mexico was supposed to be a new start. There isn't much new about it. *Wherever you go, there you are.*

She picked up her phone and texted Stacia back.

["Omg! Approved? Congratulations! Of course, Gus and I are coming!"]

Send.

She put down her phone and took Roger outside for a bathroom break. The expanse of stars never failed to pull her into their magic.

David Attenborough's voice fills the sky, "This astrophile would be drawn to the cosmos not only for their spectacular wonderment but for the possibility that among all that constant, there is potential to glimpse a small change; the glimmer of a satellite, the passing of a shooting star, or, unlikely as it might be, the death of a star."

Morgan Freeman, another voice from a distant star, replies. "David, one must consider that in the vastness of all that space, one might, with all the power of science and facts behind them, see that God is in there?"

Attenborough: "Perhaps. But this woman isn't looking for God. She is looking for change. Lily stares up at the unchanging sky, so passionately, for fear that she might miss a cosmic event. Something spectacular could occur any given second, and in that same second, would vanish."

Back inside, Lily had fallen asleep on the couch with her wine. She was awakened when Gus set his keys on the small kitchen counter. He leaned over, kissed her forehead, and took her glass into the kitchen. She sat up a little. "How was work?"

"Okay. The Albuquerque Comic Con was happening. A little bit of cosplay in the bar tonight."

"Oh. Any good ones?"

"A pretty-solid Crow. Manu Bennet, the real one, he dropped in."

"What?"

"Yeah, just for a minute. It was weird."

Lily bit her lip. "So… Chick and Stacia's adoption was approved. They are having a party and invited us to come."

Gus lit up as though Manu Bennet had just walked into the bar. "When? Do you wanna go?"

"I dunno. You said you wanted to go back to Grand Rapids. So… anyway, I told them we'd be there. It's in a couple of weeks."

"Shit. Okay. I'll see about getting my shifts covered."

"It'll be fun."

"Cool. Yeah. I want to see those guys. I think it will be awesome."

Lily shuffled up off the couch with her plush blanket. She was wearing a pair of short, silken pajama bottoms that gave Gus a rush. "I'm heading to bed," she said. This caused Gus to race through his routine so he could catch her while she was still animated. Those shorts stirred something in him, and he'd become a predator. He quickly rinsed the bar from his body and ferociously brushed his teeth. He shot himself with a small dose of his Fahrenheit cologne and slid under the sheet next to her warm body. Upon contact, Lily murmured, "No. I'm tired." Gus's body switched, as quickly as an event in the night sky, from the warm and anxious desire for love to the warm and anxious tinge of anger via rejection. The tip of him could feel the soft skin, less than an inch away, warm and smooth and inviting. He gave it a second more before exiting the bed.

"Where are you going?" Lily whispered.

"For a smoke," Gus replied while slipping through the bedroom door.

Outside, Gus looked at the same space (or was it?) that Lily had just gazed into a short while before. He took a drag off his cigarette and thought of their trip to GR. Like in bed, the excitement had the potential to let him down. There was little optimism in Gus right then. Just another lonely smoke under the stars. That loneliness led to thoughts of the past. He thought about the old Maggie's Bar that he worked at, and he thought about lost opportunities like Tina.

She can probably see the same stars from wherever she is. Maybe less so if she's in some big city. She probably is. She was such a good painter. Fuck that anyway. Art only serves as an invitation to ridicule with no reward.

He thought of her young face—her young face was all he knew, but he'd studied it so closely and on so many occasions.

Those little delicate hands, with that blue nail polish, often dirty with powder from smudging charcoal drawings. Hands adorned with all those pewter rings. That little dip where her neck meets her shoulder blades and the way her dark hair brushes against it.

He felt a tinge of sentimental-want/need run through him. He could visualize her lips parting as she worked the CD player. Her Counting Crows and her Guns n' Roses setting the soundtrack for a love story.

He went back into the house and quietly put on the record *Streetcore*. He strutted and danced back out to the patio while "Coma Girl" played in the background. His late-night energy escalated. He thought of the patches on her bag and the shape of her ears, her earrings, and the way she smirked when she rolled her eyes. He thought of the chai and the Djarums and that sugar and spice. He could taste her, briefly, as brief as a star burning out.

"Let's siphon up some gas, let's get this show on the rooooooaaaad," he sang out loud.

"What are you doing?" Lily stood in the sliding glass door, disheveled and tired.

"Nothing. Go back to bed. I'll turn it off."

He turned off the stereo while she kissed his forehead. The song was still playing in his head.

Corner Soul

Tina was browsing the bootleg cassette section in Music X, flipping through the old, worn-out, and sometimes plain old handwritten, hand-dubbed homemade cassettes. Pearl Jam, Led Zeppelin, The Grateful Dead, and on and on. She was only paying a modicum of attention until she was hit in the forehead with a brick.

تعطیلات آفتابی - Holiday in the Sun

A homemade cassette tape of the Sex Pistols *Never Mind the Bollocks* must have made its way from Iran into the United States via some soldier who'd wandered into a shop during Desert Storm or some other event. Her hands began to tremble as she pulled the cassette tape out of its case; a wave of emotion flooded her skin and bones. She closed her eyes and breathed in the dust-filled air as though, upon re-opening her eyes, this object would no longer be there.

Broken, like a window shattered by a baseball, Gus's voice yelling "Tina" struck her from a short distance. She let out her breath and looked toward him while shoving the cassette back into its slot.

"Hey, Gus."

"What's wrong?" He could sense something was going on.

"Nothing. Let's get something to drink."

At the counter, Gus ordered an Americano for himself and a chai latte for Tina.

"No chai. Americano too, please." She was a bit brash.

"Really?"

"What? You think Persians only drink chai tea, smoke Djarums, smell like spices, and taste like sugar? I'm Persian, not Indian, asshole."

"Whoa, Tina, jeez, I'm sorry."

"Never mind."

Gus, in a full-on Clash phase, asked the barista to put on *London Calling*. "Wrong 'Em Boyo" blasted around X while the two sat in their booth. Tina was looking at Gus as though she was going to eat his face, with lasers shooting out of her eyes. Gus didn't want to say anything.

"What are you smirking at?" she asked him as though he was smirking.

"Tina, what's wrong?"

"Why do you always think that something is wrong? Just like every time, nothing is wrong, dude."

Gus took a sip of his coffee and lit a cigarette. "Can I have one?" she asked.

"Not if you are going to yell at me."

She took his pack and helped herself. She lit the cigarette and held it in the air with her elbow on the table.

"Tine..."

"Tine? Who the fuck is Tine?" Her accent was thicker than usual. "When did I ever say you could call me Tine? Tine is for dumb chicks at the mall. Is that what I am to you, Gus? Am I just a dumb chick at the mall? Christ."

"Oh my fucking god, Tina." He looked at her face, focused on her reactions.

She looked down at the table and started scratching at the wood with her fingernail. She took a half-drag off her cigarette and blew the smoke up toward the ceiling out the side of her mouth. She inhaled and exhaled and looked up at Gus, saying, "I'm sorry."

"You don't have to be sorry. I mean, you kind of do. I don't want to ask you what's wrong though."

"I know. But, believe me, whatever is wrong is nothing you want to know about. Let's take a walk or something."

"Okay." Gus stood and put his hand out with the "after you" motion. She grabbed her bag and shot by him toward the door—anxious for fresh air. They walked toward downtown. Tina's walk started fast and strong, but quickly slowed its pace. Gus followed suit until she suddenly stopped and turned, and he nearly ran into her—he did bump into her. He put his hand around her arm and pulled her a little so she wouldn't fall. They both felt something in the touch. She put her hand on his. She embraced it slightly, and their skin became electric. Then, with that same defiance and rebelliousness that put them here, she shoved his hand away while looking up at him. He felt small and pathetic and wanted to run.

"Let's go," she demanded, and proceeded to walk toward the river. She found a ledge on which she sat and commanded Gus to sit. He sat. They stared at the water under the big gray sky for what seemed like an eternity. Her feet, in a pair of Vans, fidgeted a little.

Gus wanted to embrace her and kiss her and hold on for dear life. He always did have lofty goals. She wanted him next to her but wanted to be alone. She didn't want to talk. The day's life had been sucked out of her, and she had no more room for things.

After a short eternity, she looked toward Gus and paused. Nothing needed to be said; it was all in her face.

"I need to go," she said.

"I need you to stay," he said.

"Okay, but you need to buy me shawarma." She smiled a little.

"Would you like some chai with that?"

"Fuck you, Gus."

1-2, CRUSH ON YOU

Gus had a lot of time to think. Time, plus more time, plus attention deficit disorder, could easily be a ticking time bomb planted in an empty field full of scarecrows. The time bomb's clock was ticking down on the eve of that kiss. His heart was tearing under the immense pull of rapture. Every second seemed like an eternity, with little distraction at one o'clock in the morning. His eyes were sore, and his lips were dry.

Why the fuck do I not have her number? He remembered times when numbers were mentioned. Played off or pushed into one-liners about commitment or whatever. Those were little puncture wounds, but at the time, they seemed harmless. The relationship was special in its own way, and numbers seemed unnecessary or too complex. They were young, after all. Space and time were unlimited and had no bounds. A drop of rain only meant sunshine was right around the corner. *Unless you're Tina,* He thought, *She'd probably flip rain and sun.*

He lay on the floor, exhausted and spinning *Counting Crows'* "Round Here," over and over again, as though the slowing of time wasn't torture enough. Every fucking move, every fucking joke, or smirk, or smile ran through his head on repeat. What the fuck put him here?

"Round Here" plays, and something radiates. The room blurs, and his eyes struggle to stay open while his mind and heart burn. There is a void here. A wormhole in the floor. There, just out of reach, is her hand. The visual shifts into a vision of a young girl shoplifting from a jewelry shop and purchasing illegal music. A story that had come to life. He can see it as though he is there, a part of it. A part of a story she once told him in the café. He weeps deeply, and the wormhole swallows him up.

It's raining big, fat drops, and his skin is slick. He can feel her hands on his cheeks and her lips press against his. He places his hand on the back of her

     Aaron Paul Schaut

head as she pushes him against the wall. The world melts away, and they are left under the dim light, looking into each other's eyes and breathing each other's breath. They take each other's hand and step off of the sidewalk into darkness. Maybe it's a bright white light they walk into.

He walks into a coffee shop, and she hands him a drawing. He can make out her silhouette, but the face is marked up and crossed out. She's looking into his soul for a reaction. He lights a cigarette and winks. She smirks and takes the cigarette from him. They are in his car, heading west. Big dreams of Hollywood America. Why not?

Night falls and he has no more tears. His sighs have become dry and useless. He gets up to his knees and stares at the wall. Big, dumb, useless U2 poster that he then reaches up for and tears down. He turns on the television to drown out the noise. He crawls to his bed and somehow falls asleep. Perhaps because he knew he'd drive to Ann Arbor. What else could Gussy do? He was obviously smitten.

Aaron Paul Schaut

HEART & MIND

Earlier in the year. An afternoon in December of 1998.

Gus walked into a big empty bar called Diversions. The place was across the street from school, offering an easy cocktail between classes. The bartender, Michael, had a cool, pleasant demeanor that made him easy to talk to. He was always smiling and had a little bit of a lisp that made him seem even more sincere than the average bartender. In fact, he was a sincere as they come.

Gus walked into the place like he was Jack Torrance, walking in for a stiff drink and some deep talk with Lloyd the bartender—only about 20 years younger.

"Mikey! How's it going?" Gus shouted across the room like he owned the place.

"Good, Gus, what are we starting off with today?"

"I'll do a vodka tonic, my man. Try to stay light, being that it's only noon."

"He-he. You got it, buddy." He had blonde, curly hair and a big smile. "So, what's the word? Tell me what's going on in your life?"

"You know, same old." Gussy wore his problems on his face.

"So… a girl thing?" Mikey asked with a cartoonish raised eyebrow.

"A Persian."

Mikey raised his eyebrow a little higher. "Ha-ha. What?"

"Yes, Mikey, a girl thing."

"Okay, but what did you say? Did you say Persian?" Now he had a twinkle in his eye.

"Yep." Gus sipped his vodka tonic through its little bar straw.

"So it's a Persian girl problem. Honey, I feel your pain."

"Ha-ha. What?"

"My brother dated a Persian. It was rough."

"Ha! I need to hear about this."

"If you are seeing a Persian, then you definitely do. She was the real deal too. He dated her while he was in Iran. I'm not kidding. Did you ever shush her, bro?"

"Maybe. What was he doing in Iran?"

"He had a bad breakup with a girl—go figure—and it led to him joining Relief International so he could get as far away from her as possible. There was a big earthquake, and they shipped him off. He met a girl over there, and they fell in love."

"Until he shushed her?"

"Yeah… haha… no, bro. So, they dated a while. He heard a lot of stories about growing up in Iran that were pretty crazy. Like all the restrictions, arranged marriages, and dowries. Did she get out of an arranged marriage?"

"Wow, man, I'm not sure."

"You should ask her. They also had all these bans on music and art. I guess they love Americans, though. That would explain how my brother could score. I mean, clearly, I got all the good genes in the family."

"Clearly."

"The shush thing is funny too. Not really a shush, but, you know, my brother is a dick. I guess she liked to talk about all this resistance stuff all the time, and sometimes she'd get pretty upset. You know? So he would tell her to stop. The way he put it, the fury of Ahura would rise up and beat him down. She was a rebel when it came to speaking out. It was funny because Mom and Dad hated that he was with her."

"Wow. I can guess why."

"You'd probably guess right."

"So after a while, he married her. I don't know. After my parents kind of disowned him, we don't

     Aaron Paul Schaut

talk much. He calls me once in a while, but we've kind of lost touch."

"That's too bad."

"Right? I should call him."

"So, it was like that for all Iranians?"

"Yeah, man. Those hijabs and stuff are real. You'd think that was all, like, archaic shit that people didn't do anymore. But they sure do! So, what about your Persian?"

"Her name is Tina. We've been running into each other here and there."

"And… you think you have a thing for her?"

"Yeah."

"Tiger!"

"I know."

"I heard they are wild in bed. You reading 300? Xerxes is fuckin' hot."

"I… um… guess?"

"So, did you sleep with her?"

"No, dude."

"What's stopping ya? You need a motivational speech? Need a little more liquid courage?"

"Man! Jesus."

"Ha-ha. Sorry, Gus, I couldn't resist. Tell me about her."

"Awe man, I barely know her. She moved here from Iran and goes to U of M. I've been running into her, like, out of the blue at coffee shops, and we just really click or something. Like, we understand each other. Sometimes it's like only we understand each other or something. Like when people say they have their own language. But, that's not all the time. Only sometimes. Sometimes, I think I say the wrong things or something, and she gets kind of upset. I dunno, man."

"Sounds pretty good to me! Maybe not those insecurities of yours. Did you ask her?"

"Nah, when she's done talking, she's kind of done talking."

"Sounds like my ex."

"Ha-ha. Sounds like all of your exes."

"Ha-ha, right?"

"Have you guys gone out on, like, a real date yet?"

"I mean, no, but… when we hang out, it feels like a date."

"My man, Gus, you have to take her on a real date. You need to show her how you feel, bro."

"I don't know if she'll like that. She can be really hard to read sometimes."

"Are you hard to read, Gussy?"

"I don't know. Am I?"

"Wellllll, I don't think so. But I'm not that into you."

"Thanks."

"No problem. Look, trust me. You need to take her out on a date. You need to ask her out, maybe with some flowers or something, take her to a movie and dinner. She needs to know you're serious, bro."

"Yeah… Yeah?"

"I'm serious, dude. Trust me. Just don't be an asshole and don't take her somewhere for Persian food or any bullshit like that."

"We joke about that."

"Yeah, bro, cool it on the jokes for a minute. I know you too well, Gus. And… when she pulls away like that? Give her space or go all in. You're gonna have to pick one."

"Jeez Mikey, coming in here and talking to you is like having a direct line to *Dear Abby*."

　　　　　　　　Aaron Paul Schaut

"Dude, I have a *Dear Abby* scrapbook."

"Oh, fuck off."

"Dude! I'm serious!"

"I better get to my next class."

"Okay, Gus. Here if you need me."

"See ya, Abby."

"Ha-ha! Fuck off, Bro."

Silver and Gold

Late Winter. A couple of years ago.

Lily had disappeared. She was apparently in Texas and wasn't answering her phone. Gus, with the help of friends Stacia and Chick, was on a mission to understand what happened to her. He and Lily had been dating for a good stint and she gave no sign that she'd be leaving.

During this time, he'd acquired a dog, ran a guy over with his car, made some new best friends and somehow held onto his job. He drank way too much coffee and smoked way too many cigarettes and drank a little too much.

While Lily was gone, Gus was also in a spin. He questioned all of the lives and loves he'd had up to the point that he'd met Lily. He questioned his location, career, friends, everything.

He sat at Lily's small kitchen table and looked at her profile on his phone. There were no updates. He stared at the page, stared at her last post.

After a few seconds staring, he tapped on the search field and typed "Tina." It wasn't the first time he'd done this—scrolling through all those little circles of people with the name Tina–scanning for familiarity in a face. He'd seen these faces before and he'd probably see them again.

She'd left too. They had finally reached that apex when time stops and allows new lovers a second to blossom. It was so long ago but the sting had a long-term effect. Somebody who'd become a fixture in your life. A person who you connected with and looked forward to seeing and sharing with. A person who was so easy to be with. Maybe they shouldn't have kissed. He needed her in his life and ruined it. At the time, he didn't have or want anyone else. It was hard to find this. It was a miracle they'd found each other. He didn't even know if she was alive. How dumb to treat such a thing as casual. He should have had her number and she should have had his. Lily should pick up the fucking phone and Gus probably should've left this city of his years ago.

His eyes burned and the little phone screen was blurry. The dog was looking for attention and he had to go to work. *Is there really such a thing as closure?*

LET ME SHOW YOU

The same day a couple of years ago, after Gus's shift.

Gussy gave the little Detroit Tigers plush bear a pat on the head before heading out of the bar and locking up. The tips for the night were okay, and the idea of getting back to Roger and that bohemian apartment seemed good enough. He was tired, and the couple of beers he had while counting down the drawer left a warm and satisfying impression. *The sooner I get to sleep, the sooner tomorrow will come.*

He settled into bed while Scully and Mulder looked for the Jersey Devil on TV. The hunt for a devil felt familiar—considering.

Slowly, effortlessly, his eyelids fell. Darkness set in while, on the TV, a little girl, crouching in some tree roots, looked up.

Freeman: "On our journey, it's not uncommon, nor voluntary, that the human mind navigates toward the *what ifs*. Gus is in a particular state of *what if* that was brought on by a series of tragedies that trigger a series of memories. When we're trapped in a cell with nobody looking, it's in our nature to break free. Gus is far from free right now. Not only was he locked in a prison of his own making, but his warden was absent and had the key. Throughout his life, there were few people whom Gus felt free with. His mind, maybe his soul, navigates into the unknown, explores the *what ifs*."

"Fuck. Morgan Freeman? You've got to leave me alone."

"Boy, you'd better get used to me. I'm your guide on this journey and, like it or not, you need me."

"Boy? Fuck."

Gus was taken back to 1999 and to the familiarity of The Black Hole. It was bitter cold outside, and the drafts in the place made it uncomfortable to sit. He was writing in an often-forgotten journal about this and that and whatever bullshit. The place was empty, save for Alex. Alex didn't work at The Black Hole in 1999, so it was odd seeing him there—it also wasn't odd.

While writing, he kept staring up at the large print of the Eiffel Tower being constructed. He was less examining it and more staring through it. Somehow, it was an alluring void.

Lost in the photo, the bell rang on the door, snapping him out of his daydream. It was Tina. She plopped her bag down and started blowing warm breath into her cupped hands while looking at Gus. A strand of hair had fallen onto her face, and it was cute.

He stood; happy she'd shown up. "A little cold?"

"Just a little."

"I'll get you a coffee."

"Yes, please."

She sat down and took her sketchbook out of her bag. Gus, returning with her coffee, asked, "You gonna let me see that book today?"

"Not on your life," she said.

"C'mon… I know it's great!"

She fell silent and took some sips from her coffee. She turned and looked through the window. Gus made a joke about her work, and she didn't look back at him. A tidal wave of worry washed over his often-broken ego. He could sense that she was bothered or mad or hurt or something.

"What's going on? You okay?"

"Yeah."

"I've seen your work. I already know it's amazing."

"Yeah."

"Did I do this? What's going on here?"

"Look, I'm never going to be an artist, and I don't want to talk about it. What I draw is for me. I don't

      Aaron Paul Schaut

want to show you or anybody. Just drop it and let's forget this ever happened."

"Okay."

"Okay."

"But—"

"—Gus!"

"Okay."

"Gus, you know how you always tell me about American road trips and Route 66 and California?"

"Yeah."

"Can we go?"

"You want to go to California? Go on the road?"

"I am in America, I'm in school and doing everything right. I draw and paint things that I feel I'll never see or touch. It's all bullshit. I need to feel it, see it, touch it."

"Now who's being dramatic?"

"Fuck you, Gus, I'm serious!"

"Jesus, Tina, you are it for me. I run around doing this and doing that, and none of it is real. It's just me doing what I'm supposed to or what I'm told. You and me? We're real. When we talk about us, we always say we are escaping reality. That's bullshit. We are a reality. We are the reality we love, and I think I'd rather embrace it than risk losing you. I'd trade everything in for this."

"I feel the same. So we are going?"

"Let's go. I'm not forgetting the little spat we had, though."

"Asshole."

THE ROAD TO ROCK AND ROLL

They peeled out of G.R. like it was a dream. All the boring parts of the trip were somehow bypassed like one always wishes they could. "Beam me up Scotty," Gus said. "Nerd." Tina chuckled.

Route 66 was warm, Tina's feet on the dashboard while the radio played some forgotten song—no— the radio played 'I Still Haven't Found What I'm Looking For.'

It was that first night, somewhere near Tulsa that they found a hotel called Desert Hills. The woman behind the counter was robust, had a crooked smile and a jolly personality.

"Single or double?" she asked with a smirk. She winked at Gus.

"Single." Gus said, looking toward Tina for approval.

"I like you two. Tell you what, rooms on the house."

"Really? Tina asked.

"Honey, this is his dream.—I just work here. Here's your key. Room 46664. Park in front of the door.

"There's a room 46664? That seems crazy." Gus scrutinized the woman with a glare.

"Again, hun, your dream, your rules."

"Any place you recommend we eat?"

"You saw the Waffle House on your way in. Just go there. Tell them Pat sent you."

A swirling of stars carried them to Waffle House. Their Waffles were already prepared, and they sat cozy across from each other.

"Is this my American Dream Gus?" Tina smirked and bit her lower lip.

"It's definitely American."

A big woman, probably in her fifties, stood over them with a coffee pot. "Look at you. Ain't ya'll the cutest thing I ever seen sittin' in that booth. Ya'll want some coffee?

"Sure," Gus says, a little taken by her statement.

"Tell ya'll what. Be'n that ya'll are so cute and friends of Pat and all, this all on the house."

"Really?" Gus asks.

"It's his dream," Tina chuckles.

"Fo-sho!" The woman laughs heartily.

Another swirl of stars and they are in Albuquerque. The weather is warm and dry and the sky as blue as Tina's cerulean oils. They check in at the El Vado. The room was again free, and Pat runs the desk here as well.

"We must be really cute," Tina says. "We haven't spent a dime."

Gus looks at her and winks. "And the coffee has always been fresh and delicious. You notice? Also, how are we in Albuquerque? I thought we were in Tulsa."

"We were in Tulsa. Now we are here, silly."

"Don't call me silly." He frowned a little, smirked a little.

"Don't question reality, Gussy."

They walked the beach at Santa Monica. The weather was perfect, the waves picturesque, and the sand was the right kind of warm for bare feet. Tina put her hand on Gussy's arm, and the waves grew taller. She wrapped her hand around Gus's wrist, and the sun half-set and stayed that way. The waves grew taller. They breathed each other in—warm, hot—their lips just barely touching, and their eyes open so to not miss a second of each other.

Gus had become electrified at the touch. A static went through him, causing him to take her arm and pull her in tight. He gently let his fingers run from behind her ear, down her neck, and into the small pit of her shoulder blade. "I want to live here. I want to live this moment." He grabbed the back of her head, and she grabbed his. They began kissing passionately—wet, warm. The world dissolved away like somebody had painted out the scene. The two melted down into the sand while kissing. The sky became dark but filled with stars, one of them a shooting star.

There was nothing awkward about the moment.

Tina pulled them up off the sand. They stood at the foot of a bed, in a luxurious room, overlooking the Pacific. No—it was a cabin at Big Sur. Gus lowered himself down the length of her body. Inch by inch, he gently kissed and breathed on her—breathed her in. From her neck to her shoulder, to her breasts. From her breasts to her navel. His lips moved with her panties as he slid them down. He kissed the crevice between her thigh and her pelvis while she ran her fingers through his hair and along the back of his neck. He traced her lines with his tongue, inhaling, appreciating her scent while traveling around more sensitive parts of her.

He rose back up, taking nothing for granted as he stood. She kissed his neck and chest, her hands following her kisses. She looked him in the eyes, deeply, eternally.

He touched her cheek below her eye, and she traced his face with her hand.

She took his hand and lay down on the bed. There was a fire in a large stone fireplace, and the gas lamps had dimmed. She invited him to her, spreading herself. *Sheets of empty canvas.* He scanned her, as she lay like this, before accepting her invitation. *Untouched sheets of clay.* He had never felt so hard. A surge ran through his whole body.

And he entered her—slowly—nothing left for granted. They came—both—together.

They were in a mid-century modern house in Palm Springs. It was Christmas, and the decor was

     Aaron Paul Schaut

Hallmark. Gus carried a turkey to the table where Tina's young and beautiful sister and mother sat. The two sat a version pulled from a good memory—a Polaroid.

The walls of the dining room held a portrait of Gus. Its artist? Tina. Next to it, a portrait of Tina. Its artist? Gus. Both post-impressionist in style, and both wild with electric hues. Dioxazine Purple and Phthalo Blue and Cadmium Orange.

A child was on the horizon, Tina adorned by a small but noticeable bump.

Freeman: "But how could you then transgress? Would you then cease to be you?"

"Fuck off, Freeman. I like it here!"

They sat in a room full of windows. An attic studio with perfect light. Each had their own space for painting. Her hair was long and gray and soft, and his was salt-and-pepper and fluffy. Glasses perched at the ends of their noses while they painted.

Landscapes of all the places they'd seen scattered about the room. Just messy enough to be real.

Freeman: "Reality is a construct of the whole's perspective. This, what we are experiencing, is a perspective of one, or two."

"Morgan Freeman! It's exactly real—right now!"

There, with paint still wet on sheets, they made love. It was no less intense than the first time. His anticipation and her anticipation for the moment of spiritual oneness had never faded. Records, vinyl, of all the songs they'd listened to through those little split earbuds completed the room. They came, together, to the tune of "Raining in Baltimore" while canvases painted themselves. Out in the driveway: a beat-up Acura and a big, shitty Olds.

Freeman: "That's odd. Don't you think?"

He sat there, in Music X, hoping she'd return. She did. As she walked in, a guy in a polo shirt called her a name so vulgar that we won't bother writing it. Gus stood, went to him, and beat him until his

      Aaron Paul Schaut

ghost slipped through cracks in the old wooden floor.

"Freeman, that was your fault for butting in," Gussy said aloud and with a grin.

The floor of an abandoned warehouse, glow-sticks, and clear plastic beer cups, and nothing to worry about save insulting each other with the warmth of two friends. Fireflies in the summer.

Attenborough: "The firefly is a creature that has the strange ability to produce light. They bioluminesce. A female firefly judges the quality of a male's genes by the precision of his timing and the brightness of his light."

Freeman: "David, and what of Gus's timing? Gus's light?"

"Guys! Stop!"

A swirling and hum, scattered glowing lights, and an unrecognizable sound that might be a truck outside his window, Gus was jolted awake. He felt the post-dream rush of excitement and the warmth of love and the thrill of perfect lovemaking, and he was wet, and the joy of a fully fleshed out future, a lived future, and—he recognized his surroundings and…

…and what is reality? Could it be that reality is whatever you make it?

DEATH OR GLORY

He was up before the city and the sun. He had enough sense to take the time to shower and brew a pot of coffee in the small, four-cup coffee maker. He had to force the patience but needed the fresh coffee and, should he find her, to be fresh.

The cold nipped at his knuckles, and he blew into his cupped hands after unlocking the car and settling into the driver's seat.

Shit! He'd forgotten the ring. He left the car running, ran up to the house, and realized he needed his keys, so he ran back to the car and then back to the house. He had to search for the ring, as he'd been looking at it while in and out of last night's tidal winds. He looked and looked before finally realizing it was on his pinky finger. One would never expect to find a ring on their finger, I suppose.

It wasn't time yet, but there was a feeling of snow in the air. That old car started hard, as if it wanted to stay under the covers and sleep in. "Too bad, old girl," Gus said as he cranked it over.

The moon was a full one, a big bright orb in Gus's rearview while the sky ahead became ever so slightly silvery bright. He was listening to a mixtape of odd songs that included bands like U2, Tears for Fears, and other '80s pop. Some of the songs were irritating, but changing out the cassette would be a distraction from the goal at hand. Mind you, we were only 15 minutes into a 2-hour drive.

He passed the Lowell exit, the Lyons-Muir exit, and the Portland exit. The Portland exit had a gas station with a coffee refill and bathroom break. These two things go hand over fist on a drive. On through Lansing and on and on. He popped out the cassette and found some MSU station playing alternative underground. Sonic Youth counted down the drive. Ten, twenty, thirty, forty. *Tell me that you wanna hold me.* He was singing along at

 Aaron Paul Schaut

the top of his lungs while his anticipation kept building, time turning over and over and over.

The sun was a giant ball of frosty glow. She appeared white in the sky as she pulled the cover of earth off of her. His left hand on the steering wheel, he admired the ring—a skull with little obsidian eyes. And so it did start to snow. Big damp snowflakes that had almost become raindrops. They lived a short life splattering against the car's windshield and hood, the road, grass, and trees. He removed the mixtape and, from the back seat, pulled out a *Mule Variations* cassette. *Take It With Me* is where he'd left off—a kind of fitting anthem for this adventure.

Finally, Gus had made it to Ann Arbor. He'd never been here before and had no idea where she might be. The campus was vast, and the town wasn't small. He remembered her mentioning a place called Zingerman's, so he made this his first destination.

He navigated his way into the downtown area. He recognized the familiar Blind Pig, as so many bands had played there over the years. He'd heard about the Sonic Youth, REM, and Rollins shows there. Even fucking Pearl Jam. Grand Rapids' Fountain Street Church had a lot of great acts, but The Blind Pig had it beat by a landslide. *One, two, three, four, five against one, five, five,* ran through his head.

Gus decided to park the car and look around. He worked his way down Washington, where he spotted a coffee shop. His nerves twitched at the thought of walking into Sweetwaters and finding Tina sitting there. She'd probably yell at him for showing up. He hesitated at the entrance before deciding to have a smoke on the sidewalk. His hands trembled a little. The trembling was less a result of fear and more a result of anticipation or overstimulation. He flipped his Zippo and looked around. The town seemed really, really big right now. Giant even. It felt like it had thirty main streets! Somewhere in all this was Tina, tucked away, reading or drawing, and listening to something cool.

He couldn't take it anymore. He tossed his cigarette into the street and opened the door with the pull of Helios. His eyes scanned the place, but he knew she wasn't there. He didn't feel her presence. So, he made his way to the counter and ordered himself an Americano, setting himself in a chair next to the window. He watched people go by, walking their dogs, looking cold, and yearning for their morning coffee. Gus felt like a stranger among them while simultaneously feeling like he belonged there, maybe more than they did. He was, after all, the lead in a romance novel. He had a grand purpose.

Where in the fuck would she be?

GET DOWN MOSES

Present Day in Grand Rapids.

After a short night of drinks and a little catching up with Stacia and Chick, Gus and Lily, awake early because of the time difference, decided to head out for breakfast and coffee. The location of Gus's soul was not completely GPS-locatable as it traveled between dimensions and time. Sentimentality lurked even in the gravel along the roadside.

They stopped into the Black Hole and ordered the usual. That barista, Alex, was still there and still knew their drinks. The two would sit a while, waiting for the world to open up.

It was hard for Gus not to reflect on all of the versions of himself that had sat along the wall of the cafe. The place knew every iteration of him: young punk, artist, lover, friend, fanatic, obsessive and compulsive, and drowning in fear and sadness. The wall could have had marks in it, like those marks moms draw on the door frame as their children

 Aaron Paul Schaut

grow taller. Leonard Cohen was playing and had been playing for just as many years—if not more!

"What do you want to eat?" Lily asked.

"Wolfgang's, of course."

"Oh yeah. That sounds great!"

Lily was so pretty sitting there. She had a knife to Gus's throat, but that was okay. It was his problem, after all. He was weak and worn down and could never find it in himself to not be codependent in this thing. There used to be a door at the end of a journey. The journey would have hurdles and trials, but the idea of reaching that door was loaded up with desires and fire and piss and vinegar. All the things that Morgan Freeman might call "wonderments of life's little achievements" or something. It had been a hot minute since Gussy's dreams were graced by the actor and his wisdom.

Gus, attempting to avoid any more reflection, said, "Before going to eat, let's hit the antique store."

"Cool."

They hopped in Stacia's car and headed toward the big old warehouse that housed something like forty billion antiques. There were threats that this place was going to get turned into condos or something, for a long time. Nevertheless, all forty billion antiques were still there. In fact, walking into the place, it seemed like they literally were still there— all the same stuff in all the same booths. The place was void of time, frozen in place like a star sitting in the sky. There was an old giant print of Café du Monde hanging there that was still in the same faded state that it had been when it was hung some ten million years ago. It was like this place existed between two dimensions, void of gravity and unaffected by its pull.

"Antiques that served as nostalgia in the antique store have become their own fucking nostalgia. This place hasn't changed a bit!" Gus poetically pointed out, like some kind of Gandalf, after an hour or so of walking around.

     Aaron Paul Schaut

"Yeah, it's weird. Two or so years, and I still know where everything is in this place."

"I'm kinda bored, and I'm getting hungry. You wanna go?"

"Yeah, I'm starving, and the dust is getting to me."

"Yeah, me too. Let's get the fuck outta here."

The drive to Eastown was lackluster, and Gus fidgeted, not being allowed to smoke in Stacia's car. You'd think he could go 15 minutes without a smoke. Her pop music was playing, and both of them felt a little embarrassed having it on. Nobody bothered to turn it off.

They passed the art gallery where Lily used to consult. It was no longer an art gallery. She wondered what happened and felt a little bad about not keeping in touch. At least the town was still graced with Reb's artwork. It seems like he's now touched an urban object on every block! Reb cows and Reb birds and more Reb cows.

They parked the car in the usual spot in Eastown and began crossing the street with a little jaunt that says you care about traffic but not enough to run. Lily made fun of Gus's bullshit jaunt, and they were laughing when Gus looked into the Early Bird and came to an immediate stop. He saw her face, her eyes, and didn't need to see more. Her eyes were etched into his memory not as a Polaroid but as an Ilford Platinum Super Gloss print.

Gus looked at Lily, but only for a second, as he couldn't stop verifying reality. *She doesn't recognize me*, he thought, as she looked down, as he tried (as though he could) to zoom in. "She's with somebody," Gus said aloud.

"What?" Lily asked.

Gus looked at her and forced a nonchalant smile.

"Do you know her?" Lily had caught on. She always had an acute awareness of Gus's anythings.

"Yeah. Let's go say hello."

     Aaron Paul Schaut

The dumb-looking guy looked up at Gus with much fear. For Gus is a mighty God, and it would be unlikely that any human would not fear him. ;)

"Tina? Persian Tina?" Gus knew it was her, and as though no time had passed, threw in the Persian thing. Gus was proud of it anyway. Persian empire! He himself was amongst a goddess. She had become a beautiful woman. This was unexpected, or, at least, not considered. In Gus's head, she'd only ever been the young woman he knew.

Tina looked like she was going to faint. Gus thought she might run. Lily stepped up to the table and immediately started examining Tina. The dumb-looking guy with Tina stood up to greet the great Gus god.

He grunted, "Tina's husband," as he knew he indeed belonged to Tina and would be a fitting tribute for tonight's feast at the table of the gods.

After Tina and Gus made introductions to their lesser halves, Cooper, Tina's guy, asked Gus and

Lily to join them. Gus began to mumble something along the lines of "well, um, we were going to…" when Lily burst in with a "love to" while pulling out a chair. The tone in her voice may as well have spitted out, "you are fucking dead, man."

Cooper, without suspicion and knowing full well of Gus's role in Tina's life, asks questions—genuine and sincere. Lily, on the other hand, had never heard of Tina and is suspicious. She'd marked Tina as bad news already.

Tina and Gus talked about their young selves and the impact they had on each other. Lily and that guy Cooper look to each other for some kind of moral support and assurance that the whole thing is solid. All while Gus and Tina steal glances at each other with the kind of enhanced excitement and nervousness you might achieve while shoplifting. Both of them had spent plenty of time thinking of reuniting with each other and when the situation finally arrives that they do? If only it could be without those other halves. I suppose it keeps a kind of forced reality in the picture. But, neither Gus, nor

 Aaron Paul Schaut

Tina, knew what the other was feeling. Maybe the looks gave some of it away. The looks could never express all of it.

"What are you doing now?"

"I'm an artist. Gallery showings and everything." Tina rolled her eyes as she said it. Gus knew why.

Lily was struck with a sudden familiarity of Tina's face. "Oh my god, I knew I recognized you. Tina. Tina Pahlavi! I've curated your pieces for at least two gallery events."

Tina blushed.

"Ah, my famous wife." Copper said with a smile. "I'm so proud of her."

Gus squinted at Cooper. He looked back at Tina and took command of the conversation. "Holy shit, Tina! You have no idea how happy that makes me. I've waited and waited to walk into a gallery and see your work. For some reason, I always knew."

In that moment, Gus forgot that there were other people there. His heart was in his throat.

Gus let Cooper pay the bill. He had his pride, after all. Walking away, Gus stops and turns back and puts his hand around Tina's arm. That touch was it! Both of them are transported back in time toward what would be nearly the end of what we could, in hindsight, call a very important relationship. The electricity causes the lights to flicker in the cafe and Cooper and Lily duck and cover for fear of earthquakes. "It's okay," Tina says. Gus, unflinching, asks for her number. *I'll be damned if I'm losing touch with you again,* he thought. "Maybe this time we keep in touch?" he says.

Tina, pulling away a little and still in the same shock as Gus says "Um, well."

"I mean exchange numbers? We can text sometimes. Facebook? Instagram?" So bold, Gussy, asking for her number right there in front of Lily and this other guy.

     Aaron Paul Schaut

Gus and Lily stumble off of the curb while Gus looks back at Tina. "You've got to be kidding me," Lily says.

"What?" Gus replies.

Tina looked back at him too.

Gus, in his head, must have put fifty different scenes together where he finally runs into Tina. None of those scenes played out even remotely close to how this one did. This was dark comedy, fucking Shakespeare—this was God-style torture. It was almost worse than not running into her at all. Or was it?

Gus started the car. Lily was quick to change the station and *Thunderstruck* was playing on the radio and Gus lit a cigarette.

"You can't smoke in here. What is wrong with you?"

"*Fuck.*" Gus smiled.

A guy holding a cardboard sign that read in crude marker, "SHE GOT AWAY" stood there on the sidewalk, gawking at Gus and signaling that he needed a cigarette. Nope! Gussy was busy.

Ramshackle Day Parade

The drive back to Stacia and Chick's place was a little uncomfortable to say the least. Gus wanted terribly to have some time to himself, to look at Tina's number in his phone and think about what all of this meant to him. Lily was jealous and angry but deflected and talked about Tina's art. Gus kept deflecting by talking about the adoption party. "We need to bring a gift!" he pulled into the liquor store off Fulton and Diamond. Gus pulled a bottle of Jameson off the shelf.

"You're not getting that," Lily grunted.

"It's a gift," Gus replied, fake grin on his face.

"Who the fuck brings a bottle of Jameson to an adoption party? Come on, we're going somewhere nice."

They ended up at a small store selling hand-crafted or locally sourced baby things.

"I don't know anything about babies," Gus mumbled under his breath.

Lily pulled a cute little onesie off of a rack and grabbed a pair of baby-sized Chucks off of a shelf. "They can return them if they don't fit."

"Little tiny Chuck Taylors," Gus smiled.

They paid for the gifts and headed back to the car.

"So, how come you never told me about Tina?" Lily finally asked the question that Gus had been preparing for.

"Tell you what? It was a long time ago. We were really very good friends."

"You never talk about your friends."

"I haven't seen her or talked to her for like twenty years. She lived in Ann Arbor and we'd see each other at coffee. One day she just quit coming to G.R. and we lost touch. I don't know why."

"Hmm." Lily responds. "Give me a cigarette."

     Aaron Paul Schaut

"You quit."

"I don't care. Give me one."

He reaches for his pack and hands it to her. Lighter too.

"I wish you would have told me about her, Gus. You never tell me anything."

"What?" Gus rolls his eyes. "I never thought to. Why would I?"

"I could tell, Gus. I could tell you had a thing."

Morgan Freeman: "Fortunately for Gus, they had arrived at friends, Stacia and Chick's house. That knot that had formed in the pit of Gus's stomach was as tight as a knot could be. Without reflection, his insides might burst from its sheer force. Spending any more time talking about it with Lily, would only add a second knot. A double-knot, so to speak."

"Let's do this," Gussy said while giving a look that implied he didn't want to talk about it anymore.

They walked up the steps to the porch, all decorated with balloons and streamers, and let themselves in. They could hear the voices of several people traveling through the hallway and into the entryway. Both of them felt a bit disconnected from their friends and it stung.

Walking into the kitchen, Jesse, a long story, was the first to see Gus and Lily. He ran up and hugged Gus and shook Lily's hand. "Good to see you, man."

Then, as if a train had slammed on its breaks, Stacia's voice carried through the room. "Oh my god! Gus, Lily! Come and meet Luna!"

Gus and Lily made their way toward the kitchen table. They were looking for a baby. Instead, they were looking at a girl who appeared to be about 10 years old. The disconnect between their friends felt really real.

"You have… a teenager," Lily said with a bit of confusion in her voice. "Nice to meet you, Luna."

Gus shook the young girl's hand but was only half-present. He was still thinking about what had happened at the Early Bird. He couldn't shake the gut-wrench and how beautiful she was. He couldn't disconnect. Lily had sat down at the table next to Luna and their voices echoed around the room. Gus let himself out for a smoke.

On the porch, Gus lit a cigarette and stared at her name in his phone. This meant so much to have her there. So many times he'd messaged or called Lily over "the disappearance" and he felt this would lead to a similar result. Something along the lines of, "The person you are trying to reach is unavailable. After the tone…" Gus was all too familiar with that tone. It may as well have been a weekly air raid test siren in a town that had seen a past war. A little jolt for everyone.

Somebody slammed the door behind them and it caused Gus to jump. In that moment, he'd accidentally dialed Tina. He could hear her voice, "Hello?" His heart went into arrhythmia. An anxiety-driven response, he put the phone to his ear. "Tina!"

"It's me. What do you want?"

He was slightly crushed that she was so spicy in her reply. Without thinking, and with the entire weight of the world on his toe, he said, "I'm at the Tip Top. Can we meet?" It was only afterward that he realized that he wasn't at the Tip Top and would find it nearly impossible to meet. The monthly severe weather test siren rang out while Gus tried to parse the cause from the effect of the situation. Indeed. A storm was brewing. He thought of Lily's departure and just started walking. Tip was only 4 blocks away. He can't remember the conversation because his mind was buzzing. All he needed to hear was, "I'll be there."

Stay Free

Late 1998

It was the third or fourth time they met. Who's counting? Another life, another universe. Maybe they'd never met. Maybe they knew each other well, across the vast distance of the universe they were bound. Maybe they only connected on the surface or maybe they connected on some deeper level. A Twin Flame, they call it, though not popular at the time.

Gus was frustrated by a teacher at school. The teacher was brash and as an artist, had no business teaching the craft. He sat at a table in The Black Hole wishing he could be transported to another body. Some life without art school and disheveled brooding peers commending each other for their artist mentalities. Yup! To be an artist, you must resign to a life of grief and sadness or one cannot possibly create art. Such bullshit. *Posers.* Gus was no different though. Was he not brooding and contemplative and sad? Sure he was—artsy fuck.

Tina walked in and Gus stood up as though he knew she was coming. She didn't say anything and simply plopped her bag down on the table and sat down, she puffed a breath as she sat, her lips and cheeks expanded while looking up at him with a slight eyeroll. He smiled and walked over to the counter and ordered her a coffee.

Back at the table, he asked her "what's wrong?"

"You always ask me what's wrong. So, classes are so dumb. Then, I wanted to come here to get out and there was an accident and it took me like a million years to get here. Crappy car."

"I like your car!"

"I'm glad somebody does."

"I'm glad you made it."

"Good for you. You want a prize or something?"

"What's the prize?"

"I dunno, Gus. Whatever you want. I don't care."

Morgan Freeman: "The term spicy was not a popular slang term at the time. If it were, Gus would have thought her spicy. She was, indeed, full of spice."

"How about you let me look at your sketchbook."

"No way, dude. Stay out of my things."

"Come on! Are there any drawings of me?"

She rolled her eyes.

"Why don't you share the work?"

"Because it's not where I want it to be. It probs sucks anyway."

"Probs?"

"I don't know. Shut-up."

He was flirting. Maybe.

She was flirting too.

Gus had seen her work over her shoulder. Only glances of it The little he saw put him on the floor.

That brash teacher of his could probably learn a thing or ten from a simple sketch out of Tina's book. They were figure drawings—what he saw. Delicate figures somehow slightly disjointed— enough to only feel an anguish in their texture, curves, and shading.

Eventually he'd get her to let him have a look. Maybe. If she wasn't feeling spicy.

REDEMPTION SONG

Gus sat at the bar with a whiskey. He hadn't told anyone he was leaving the party. The band, London's Burning, a Clash cover band, was setting up on Tip's small stage. He felt stupid for telling her to meet him here. He should have said Black Hole, but instinct pushed him toward a drink. He didn't expect her to show up anyway. Part of him hoped she wouldn't. Most of him hoped she would.

"Hey, stranger."

Gus shut his eyes at the sound of her voice. He closed them tight and held his breath. His throat felt like it had stopped working.

He opened his eyes, breathed in deeply, stood, and looked at Tina. He'd already become accustomed to her age. She had imprinted on him, and it was easy. He put an arm around her in a half-hug. He hated himself for that. If there was ever a time to let go of boundaries, this was it. Maybe he was trying not to mess up whatever weird, delicate thing was happening between them.

He was dressed like Negan from *The Walking Dead*. She was dressed for a gender reveal party.

"I thought you'd have gotten all the drinking out of your system when we were kids," she smirked.

"I don't believe you. What brings you to the graveyard of broken dreams?" Gus, the poet.

"Do you ever think of me?" she asked.

Did he ever think of her? "You know, I've looked for you on and off for years. I always wondered if I'd step into the Black Hole and find you sitting there. I always pictured you there, just like you were then. I have you etched in my memories. You were gone. Where did you go?"

"Just… life, I guess?"

"Just life, eh? I get that. I have been chasing after life for as long as I can remember. Now I long for that feeling. Now I dream about the days when we were silly and angry and laughed at the silliest things." He exhaled slowly.

"I think we were just scared. Just young and stupid." She smiled a little. She was deflecting. It felt natural to here her deflect. She was the same Tina.

"Yeah, well, maybe… maybe we're still stupid, just older." Gus's response was natural. Same old Gussy.

"Speak for yourself, dude."

After a few long seconds, she asked, "You know, after that night… I didn't want to see you again. I… I liked you a lot back then, and I was afraid you didn't feel the same."

"Wish you had said something." He wanted to run away with her right then and there. He probably would have.

Although Gus had recently gone through the tragedy of losing Lily, this felt different His emotions were those of a twenty-year-old. He felt anxious, rebellious, and wanted to scoop Tina up and run, or else she would leave, and he would die. It felt dramatic, impulsive, obsessive, and exciting. All those feelings and emotions that had diminished over time, were reawakened. He wanted to throw up from all of his nerves tingling and neurons firing, trying to hold on so tightly to composure.

"So, what's your life like now?" she asked him, shifting the subject. She didn't want to, but the slope was slippery, and they were spiraling.

"Playing the boyfriend in New Mexico," he said before launching into a spiel about floating around and waiting for something to happen. He was complaining, and he felt it, and it was not what he wanted to be doing. He let it all get under his skin—the chasing, the worrying, the clawing at the door. All of it led to a lackluster life and an underlying feeling that he had lost time. It hurt him when she said, "That's so you," in response to his whining. This was not who he wanted to be. It wasn't her fault. It was his own sacrifices and self-deprecating nonsense. He had become so reluctant to embrace life—lead the life instead of chase it. She was right when she said it. He was probably chasing right now. It was "so Gus."

"What about you? Looks like you've got it all figured out."

"That's not fair, Gus," Tina's voice cracked with emotion. "Since graduating, I've accomplished a lot. All of it I worked my ass off for. Do you remember when I told you how I came to be in this country? Do you remember what it took? I know we didn't talk about it much, but you should have heard me when we did. Since then, everything I am and was, is me! Now, I'm stuck, and I think it's you. It's YOU I've been trying to paint, and YOU I've been trying to find. I've been stuck in a moment in time. A part of me is still there… with you!"

Gus stared into her face. He was listening intently, trying hard not to break down. He should have heard her. He thought he did. Maybe he did. "Whatever we did or didn't do, it's what made us.

It was simple and complicated and all of those things we needed at the time. Around each other, we were on autopilot. You're right, though… I'm not listening now. I'm blaming you for leaving and blaming myself for acting like a damn fool. Seeing you now, it's like restarting a mixtape right where you turned it off all those years ago. The tape is a little worn out, and the audio is a little warbly, but you still know the order of the songs and can still sing all the words."

"Jesus, you haven't changed."

"I don't have my blazer."

"That motorcycle jacket is a step down."

"Lily knows you. How long has she known your work?"

"Shit. That's weird."

"It'd be really weird if we had your art on our walls."

     Aaron Paul Schaut

"It wouldn't surprise me if you didn't notice the work hanging there. It's probably in your bedroom."

His hand inched closer and closer to hers. It was intentional, and with each inch, the space between them grew more electric. He made the connection. She dug a nail into the bar's wood, but she didn't pull away. He stared deeply into her.

"I should go," Tina said, aware of what could happen—hoping he'd beg her to stay. He would, but didn't believe she was leaving.

She leaned in to kiss him on the cheek. He turned, and their lips met. He wrapped his hand around the back of her head, hit play on that mixtape. The kiss deepened, passionate, and was the most natural thing in the world.

Maybe they'd finally found their home.

"Shit! What am I doing?" Tina pulled away.

"You were kissing me."

"Right? Shit!"

"I'm sorry, Tina."

"Me too."

She pushed him. He pulled her in. The band played "Rock the Casbah"… twice.

46664

The night continues.

The band shouted, "London's Burning," to the screams of five or six drunk punk rockers. They launched into *Police & Thieves* as one guy stumbled up next to Gus, gripping his chair and wobbling while trying to order a PBR. Tina smiled—a smile like the ones they used to share in the past when they teamed up to make fun of people.

"Did you know," Gus said to Tina, loud enough for the guy leaning on his chair to hear, "that Gillian Anderson was kind of the beginning of the punk rock scene in Grand Rapids?"

"Oi!" the little punk dude yelled. He looked to be about fifty years old. "Fuck her!" He lifted his new beer in the air.

"Fuck her!" Gus shouted.

"Yeah, fuck her!" Tina joined in, lifting her drink in the air. She and Gus nearly fell off their chairs laughing. It was a set-up.

The little punk dude went back over to the stage to sing along and stomp around.

"You wanna go outside?" Gus asked.

"One kiss, and you're already asking me outside?"

"It was a good kiss." He winked and led the way to the side door.

Gus lit them each a cigarette and smiled. She smiled back. Neither needed to say anything because the rhythm of the moment was exactly the same as it had always been. Her—a little girl in a hoodie, boots fresh out of Tehran. Him—scrappy, tall guy with a leather blazer and a dumb Yooper accent. They navigated an uncharted connection on this sidewalk, together now, as they always had.

"It's a lot easier to ignore reality, you know?" she said, looking down at her shoes.

He smiled. "It's less easy when it becomes its own reality, I guess."

"Honestly, Gussy, my sweet Gussy, I have a reality, and so do you. We need to get back to it, ya know?" She smirked, mocking his American Yooper accent a little.

Gus smiled and looked down.

"You have my number," Tina said. "You can call me sometime. Just warn me first."

Gus dug into his pocket. He muttered, "You forgot something," and pulled out that old skull ring with the obsidian eyes that she'd left in his bed all those years ago. In that moment, reality shifted, the lines blurred. Gus smiled that big crooked, goofy smile he'd carried around his whole life.

She had a tear in her eye. "Call me sometime," she said, then turned to walk away.

A quarter of a block and she turned a corner, and her phone buzzed. It was a text from Gus. It was a wink and said, "Talk to you later ;)"

THE MAGNIFICENT DANCE

On his way to Ann Arbor, a little over a day after they kissed, Gus stopped in Portland to get some coffee and use the restroom. This was at approximately 7:30 a.m.

That same morning, at 7:20 a.m., Tina had stopped at the same gas station to gas up her car. At 7:30, she was at a stop sign near the entrance to the highway as Gus entered the gas station parking lot. There was no way he could have seen her, and no way she could have seen him.

What was she doing? She was heading to Grand Rapids, where she'd sit patiently in their coffee shops, waiting for him to walk through the door. He wouldn't. He had been hitting every coffee shop in Ann Arbor, hoping to find her.

Epilogue

A trade wind, traveling across a vast sea, billowing my sail.
May we both reach our strange but familiar destinations.

Writing a story can be intensely immersive. We become our characters and live their experiences, and this particular story actually has a counterpart. Neda Aria's *Counting Crows* is the story of our Tina, who was initially inspired by author Neda Aria after she had read the first *These Americans* book. While writing these stories—while assuming your characters' identities (or maybe they are assuming yours)—you end up creating new memories, both from the vivid text and during the writing journey that, in this case, we both shared.

Through the writing, I have come to know and love Neda in more ways than I ever thought possible. I so greatly cherish who we have become, what we have created, and this dear friendship. These characters, though fictional, have become real to me, and I eagerly look forward to the next chapter in both their journeys and ours.

     Aaron Paul Schaut

BREATHE

He only had visions of what she wanted him to see.

Pictures in black and white left so much room

    for that imaginative color.

Silvertone would do,

    I suppose.

He wanted to kiss her shoulder first,

    then the neck.

He'd made this clear,

    unsure why.

This would follow the feeling of her cheek against

    his bare chest

        her breathing

            on his skin

He wants to be unclothed at all times—forever.

A breeze on a hot summer day should arouse

so easily

something within him.

The moon removes the color from the scene.

Silvertone will be just fine

I guess.

You can find the color when you dream.

You can search and explore any wet little nook you'd like, she said.

When you dream, she said.

No… He wants to be naked. A salty swim.

Warm water.

Warm breeze.

Cool air so to enhance the arousal.

He likes that she liked the breathing scene.

Hard and intoxicating like nothing else

he'd imagine, anyway.

Vivid oils with brilliant names

coloring in the Silvertone

would be just fine.

After all, it was nighttime.

Nobody could see them fucking in Silvertone.

He imagined, anyway.

The sweat served a reminder.

Imagine that.

ABOUT AARON

Born in Escanaba and now living in Grand Rapids, Michigan, he draws inspiration from personal experiences and life events. His These Americans series explores themes of identity, belonging, anxiety, and peace. His novellas Bricks, Lucid America, and now Lover's Rock continue where These Americans leaves off.

aaronschaut.com